Laban Hill

XTREME MYSTERIES

#8 Total White Out

Laban Hill

HYPERION PAPERBACKS FOR CHILDREN
NEW YORK

Laban Hill

"Okay, okay." Natalie Whittemore held up her hands to get her friends' attention. "Listen to this."

Her friends waited. They were standing at the front register of the Book Worm, the bookstore Nat's parents owned.

Everyone in the checkout line turned, too.

She took a deep breath. "Give up a big hand for my boy, Jamil Smith! He's the sickest, most amped out, bent rider in the competition." Her voice was deep and very excited.

Thud.

"Don't blink or you might miss his 1080 Roast Beef Air."

Thud thud thud.

Nat put down the pen she was using as a microphone. "So, what do you think?" She raised her eyebrows and looked expectantly at her friends, Jamil Smith, Kevin Schultz, and Wall Evans.

1

Thud.

"1080?" Wall replied. "What's that? Three 360s? This isn't figure skating, you know."

Nat laughed.

"I can't wait to see Jamil do it," Kevin cracked.

Someone on the line started clapping.

"Ewan, I didn't know you were here," Nat said, surprised.

Ewan McKendrick was the raddest inline skater in Hoke Valley, Colorado. He held up a magazine. "I'm getting a mag." Because of Nat, the Book Worm had the best selection of cool sports mags in Hoke Valley. "So what are you talking about?"

Thud thud thud.

"Jamil, could you give it a rest?" Kevin said.

Jamil smiled sheepishly. "Sorry." He put the baseball he was bouncing on the bookstore's counter in his backpack.

"It's a little early for baseball season, you know," Wall added.

"Yeah, but I found it under my bed this morning," Jamil shrugged. "I tossed it in my backpack."

Nat turned back to Ewan. "We've started a snowboarding club at school and are going to sponsor a competition at Hoke Valley's new half pipe."

"Excellent!" Ewan replied. "Can I enter?"

Nat looked at her friends.

They nodded.

"Sure. We were going to keep it to just our school,

but we could include the high school, too," said Nat. The crew went to Hoke Valley Middle School. Nat, Wall, and Kevin were in eighth grade, while Jamil was in seventh.

"No prob," Wall added. "The more the merrier."

"Whatever help you guys need, just let me know," Ewan said. He paid for his magazine. "Later, dudes." He left the store.

"We've got a lot to do, guys," Kevin reminded everybody.

"Don't sweat it," Nat replied. "I pulled off the Bear Claw last year, didn't I?" The previous spring Nat had designed and prepped the trail for the Bear Claw mountain bike race in the valley.

"Not without major help from us," Jamil said.

Nat ignored Jamil's comment and pulled a sheet of paper from her pocket. "The way I see it, this competition will be the perfect event to launch our club. Everyone will want to join." When Nat, Jamil, Kevin, and Wall returned from the Winter X Games the previous month, they had decided to start their own snowboarding club and promote their own competitions in Hoke Valley.

"Good point," Kevin replied.

"And I've made out this to-do list and divided up the jobs," Nat continued.

"Here we go," Wall cracked. "Nat is ready to run the world."

They all laughed.

"Hey, I'm getting a bum rap," Nat protested. She

suffered a lot of ribbing from her friends for being super-organized, but she didn't really mind the jokes. She knew her friends recognized her talent for organizing things.

"Could you move someplace else?" asked Nat's dad, Jake Whittemore. He waved his hand at the ten people standing in line at the register. The X-crew was definitely in the way. "I've got customers to help here."

"Sorry, Dad," Nat said. The crew retreated to the back of the store. As they passed the magazine rack, they spotted Ian Atkins.

"Hey, Ian," Wall called. "You going to enter the snowboarding competition?"

"Wouldn't miss it," Ian answered. Ian was a super-good BMXer, but in the winter he rode a snowboard like every other kid in the valley. "I'm totally stoked!"

At the back of the store, Nat's younger sister Ella was reading at a table. She had her book spread open on the table and was so lost in the story she didn't notice her sister and friends had come over.

"Could you move, Ella?" Nat asked.

"Agh!" Ella screamed. She put her hand over her heart. "You scared me, Nat."

"We need the table," Nat deadpanned.

"Nat, you've got to read this cool book," Ella said excitedly.

Nat turned to her friends and rolled her eyes.

"It's the newest Mighty Thompson Triplets mystery," Ella explained.

"Not right now, little sis," Nat replied. "We've got important club business to take care of."

"Really? Can I help?" Ella said.

"No," Nat said.

"Well, I'm not leaving," Ella replied. She crossed her arms and sank into the chair. "I was here first."

"Sisters," Wall said, exasperated. "I'm glad I'm an only child."

"Why don't you let her join us?" Kevin asked. "If my sis wanted to, I'd let her."

"No," Nat snapped. "She'd only get in the way." Then she turned toward the front of the store. "Dad! Ella's bothering us!"

"I was here first!" Ella shouted to her dad.

"You two have to work it out yourselves," Mr. Whittemore called back. "Natalie, you have to learn to get along better with your sister. I'm getting tired of you two always fighting."

"Humph." Nat sat hard in the chair on the opposite side of the table. Jamil, Kevin, and Wall grabbed the empty chairs. Ella smiled and closed her book.

"So what's your plan, Nat?" Jamil asked.

Nat flattened her paper on the table. "I still can't believe we're going to do this," Nat said, looking excitedly at her friends and ignoring her sister. "This is much cooler that just helping out on the Bear Claw."

"This was such a great idea, Jamil," Kevin said.

Jamil was the one who came up with the idea of the competition to launch the club. "Well, it wouldn't have happened if my dad hadn't put in the half pipe this year," Jamil answered. Jamil's dad, Ned Smith, was the mountain manager of the Hoke Valley Ski Resort. In the past his dad had been down on snowboarding, but last spring

Jamil had shown him that snowboarding was pretty cool.

"What's the meeting about?" Mitch Richards asked, as he and Mark Kirsten sat in a couple of empty chairs.

Wall froze. Mitch had been one of his first friends when he moved to Hoke Valley, but they had had a falling out since then. And Mark and Wall never got along after Wall beat him out in a design contest last summer. Wall won a ton of cool skateboarding stuff that Mark thought *he* deserved to win.

"We're planning a snowboarding competition," Nat explained. "You want to help?"

Mitch and Mark looked at each other.

"Uh, naw," Mitch answered. "I've got too much homework."

"Me, too," Mark said. "But can we enter?"

"Sure. We're going to announce it at school tomorrow," Kevin said.

Mitch and Mark retreated to another part of the store.

Kevin unzipped his backpack and pulled out a tall trophy with a figure riding a snowboard. "How about this?"

"Wow!" the crew exclaimed.

Kevin smiled and nodded. "My dad helped me get this. We can award it to the winner."

"Which will be me," Jamil butted in.

"No, me!" Wall interrupted.

"Not a chance," Nat laughed. "We can't organize the event, run it, and compete at the same time. People will think the competition is fixed."

"Yeah, you're right," Kevin said. He slid the trophy away. "Besides, you lame-o's know I would win."

They all protested and laughed together.

"Hey! What about me and my friends?" Ella interrupted. "Can we compete?"

"No," Nat answered curtly.

Kevin gave Nat a surprised look. "Didn't you just invite high-schoolers to compete?"

"Yeah, but that's different," Nat tried to explain. "She's just a little kid. She won't even be able to make it up the wall of the pipe."

"Will too!" Ella replied angrily. She held her book tightly to her chest.

Nat looked at her list.

"Sorry, Ella." Kevin shrugged. "We all have to agree and it looks like your sister isn't going to budge."

Ella looked disappointed. She started to open her book, but then stopped. "You guys got to read this book. It's *The Mighty Thompson Triplets and the Mystery of the Stolen Statue*."

"I've divided up the chores," Nat ignored her sister.

"Wait a sec," Ella said, "I was talking."

"Oh, sorry," Nat replied. She looked at her sister impatiently and held out her hand as if to prompt her to finish.

Ella glared at Nat. "I was saying that this mystery is really cool. An important statue in the school's library is stolen and the triplets have to find it, just like you guys do." Ella was referring to the fact that Nat, Jamil, Wall, and Kevin were crack sleuths. They had solved a number of awesome mysteries and were always on the lookout for new ones.

"Okay, Ella, that's interesting, but we've got work to do." Nat spoke to her little sister like she was a baby.

Ella slammed her book closed and left.

"Finally," Nat sighed.

"You were pretty hard on her," Kevin said. "She wasn't bothering us."

Nat glared at Kevin for a second. "She's a sister. No matter what she does, she's a pest. It's in her job description."

"Remind me not to get on your bad side," Jamil said. "Now, what have you planned?"

Nat went back to the paper. "Okay, here's the deal. Jamil and Wall hit on the local stores for contest prizes, while Kev and I work with Jamil's dad on prepping the pipe."

"That's it?" Wall said.

"That was easy," Jamil added. "Let's ride."

"You kids still snowboarding?" a voice boomed from behind the stacks.

The crew looked up. It was Bob Williams, a skiing legend in Hoke Valley. Bob had set up the first rope tow decades earlier and then sold it to the company that built the Hoke Valley Ski Resort. He had also been an Olympic skier back in the forties and had spent his life involved with the sport. He hated snowboarding.

"Hi, Bob," Kevin replied. "How's your leg?"

Bob stomped his foot. "Good as new." The previous

spring he had broken his leg skiing and had blamed snowboarders for his accident. When the crew proved snowboarders didn't cause his accident, Bob wasn't too happy. "I've been skiing without any problems."

"Good," Nat said. "We'll catch you on the mountain, Bob. We've got to jet."

Bob turned back to the shelves as the crew headed for the front of the store.

"Your father is pretty angry at you, young lady," Nat's mother, Wendy Whittemore, called to her daughter as she and her friends passed the cash register.

"What did I do?" Nat asked.

"He said you were treating your sister horribly," Mrs. Whittemore answered.

"She deserved it," Nat said.

"He had to run some errands before the stores closed," Mrs. Whittemore continued. "But he'll want to speak to you tonight."

"Oh, great," Nat groaned. "Well, I'm going out for one more run down the slopes before dark. I'll prepare myself for later."

Mrs. Whittemore waved and then turned to her next customer.

"Hi, Mr. Mack," Jamil called.

Othello Mack was at the register buying a book. He grunted a hello as he pulled money out of his wallet.

Kevin swung the door open and a cold wind whipped into the store.

Outside, Jamil turned to his friends with a funny look

on his face. "I don't want to get paranoid or anything, but did you notice who was in the store?"

"Who?"

"Just everybody who has been a suspect in the mysteries we've solved in the last year," Jamil answered. He buried his hands in his jacket pocket. The freezing cold air felt like a slap in the face. "First, we run into Ewan. Remember we thought he was behind the football sabotage?"

"But he wasn't," Nat quickly reminded him.

"Yeah, but listen to this. Next we see Ian, who we thought was behind the Bear Claw mess. Then Mitch, who we thought was ruining snowboarding on the mountain. And Mark, who we suspected of trying to blame Wall for graffiti."

"And Bob!" Wall said excitedly. "You guys thought he was trying to get rid of snowboarders on the mountain."

"That's right," Jamil said.

"And Mr. Mack, who we also suspected of sabotaging the Bear Claw," Nat said. "But so what?"

"The 'so what' is that it is just weird—" Jamil suddenly stopped talking mid-sentence. He pointed up the street.

Phil Speck was walking down the street. Phil had also been a suspect in one of their mysteries.

"This is *too* weird," Jamil replied.

"It's just a coincidence," Nat replied. "Besides, none of them turned out to be the culprits. Let's go ride. It's getting dark."

11

"Is this like a sign, or something?" Jamil continued. "It's such a coincidence, like a bad omen."

"This is a small town, that's all," Kevin reassured his friend. "There's nothing weird going on."

"Well, let's just be extra careful. I don't want anything going wrong with the snowboarding competition," Jamil warned. "You know my dad is still a new convert. He could easily hate the sport again and close down the pipe."

3

Kevin clicked into his snowboard. It had a radical six meter sidecut. Until this year nobody could handle a board built like this, because it caused riders to turn too fast. Now the sidecut had been toned down so that riders could turn fast and hard without losing control.

"That puppy's a carving machine," Jamil said, admiring Kevin's board. Jamil was sitting on the ground strapping his boots in. He didn't have click-ins like Kevin. They made it possible for Kev to just step onto his board and ride.

Kevin smiled. "Yeah, it makes all other boards wanky." Kevin always had the coolest equipment because his parents owned Alpine Sports, the best sporting-goods store in town.

Nat and Wall were also strapping their boards on. Sitting, they both spun their boards around and rolled onto their hands and knees. They pushed themselves to a standing position.

Jamil flopped onto his stomach like a walrus and got up.

"Follow the leader!" Kevin called to his friends. This was one of the crew's favorite games. One of them led and everyone else had to follow, doing the same tricks as the leader.

Kevin turned his board toward the fall line.

The trick to the game was to lead the others through as many unexpected parts of the mountain as possible, doing as many unexpected moves as possible. This was hard since all four of them could ride this mountain blindfolded and were amazing snowboarders.

Still, Kevin was the best at this game. As he made his first carve, he squared his shoulders like he was heading straight for the woods. He cut a beautiful tail of snow high into the air behind him. It was the perfect camouflage.

Nat and Wall were right on his heels, blinded by the spray. Jamil, however, hung back. He liked to leave a little space between him and the leader to give him time to react.

Kevin was ten yards from the woods, then nine, then eight. He threw his left shoulder uphill and his board followed. He came off a mogul and caught enough air to 180 to fakie. As he landed, he cut in the opposite direction. Then he turned his board straight down the fall line.

Nat was used to Kevin's tricks and she pulled off the 180 effortlessly. The same with Wall. Since Jamil rode fakie, he 180'd to regular. Kevin wasn't going to catch them so easily.

14

Kevin glanced over his shoulder and saw his friends right behind him. He smiled because he knew his friends wouldn't be expecting his next trick. He turned toward a low ridge and flew off it. He tweaked a quick Indy Air and landed in the deep pillowy snow just at the edge of the forest. They had never done that before.

His board took him deep into the woods.

Nat bounced off the ridge. She came down easy on the snow and searched the shadows for Kevin's line. Wall hucked big air as he came off and nearly landed on a branch. Luckily, he missed it.

"Aggghhh!" Jamil screamed as he hurled toward the ridge. He had carved a sharper turn and was coming at the ridge from a slightly different angle. From his view it looked like he was riding right into the trees. But once he caught air, he could see the deep powder below. He breathed a sigh of relief. His knees cushioned his landing. Then he pulled up. "Where'd they go?" He had fallen too far behind his friends and lost them.

He scanned the trees for any sign of them.

A flash of green. The kind of green that would never exist in winter. The color green that Kevin's jacket was.

Jamil followed it and immediately picked up his line. He was going to have to do some major boarding to catch up.

"Come on! This is too easy!" Nat called to Kevin. They were threading through tall pines toward a wooden bridge that led across a gap to the back side of the mountain.

Kevin went left of the bridge and hucked the gap.

15

Nat's eyes bugged out as she watched about four feet of snow collapse into the stream. The gap was now eight feet wide instead of four.

She did what any rider with brains would do. She sat down. No way was she going to try to jump that gap.

"Whoa!" Wall yelled, as he cut right and slid over the bridge. His board chattered on the icy boards. He slowed to check on Nat.

Nat waved him on. She unstrapped her back foot and stood.

The sound of snow being carved filled the air. Jamil came around a tree.

"Bridge!" Nat yelled to him.

He nodded and shot across the bridge without slowing.

Nat brushed the snow off her pants. Then she skated across the bridge with one foot still strapped to her snowboard. On the other side, she sat on a berm and buckled her back foot back on.

The trail was a slight incline so Nat couldn't pick up speed to catch up to her friends. She had to slide slowly through the woods until she reached the wide trail that her friends had taken out of the woods. By now they were so far ahead that she decided to head straight down the slope to the lodge and wait there. She'd already lost the game and their tracks were hopelessly lost among those of other riders and skiers.

Lolo's Ridge was down this way, so Nat decided to catch some air off it. She approached the jump by swinging wide to the left to slow her speed. Then as she came across the top of the ridge, she turned downhill and shot off the lip, pushing her rear foot to the left and twisting to the right. Her air time seemed like forever, but it only lasted a second. Just enough time to pull off a 360 tail grab.

Her hand dragged as she landed. It steadied her, keeping her upright as she found the edge of her board.

Nat's heart pounded excitedly. Her face was plastered with a huge grin. Snowboarding was one of two things that made her feel this good. The other was mountain biking.

The sun was beginning to set behind the mountain. Dusk was settling in the valley, which meant it was time to wrap the riding up. She knew she'd meet her friends in the lodge, so that's where she headed.

Inside the lodge, Nat skipped her usual perch beside the huge hearth fireplace. She ignored the after-ski crowd that was warming from the slopes. Instead, she went straight for their backpacks, which they had left by the lockers one floor down. She wanted to check on the trophy.

On the way she saw Bob Williams. He was talking to Jamil's dad, Ned Smith. Bob laughed so loud that he could be heard across the room. Both men were standing by the big picture window that looked out on the slopes. They must be telling skiing stories, Nat thought. Bob was like that. He loved to talk about the good old days. As if the present days could never match up. This always struck Nat as strange because these days seemed so exciting. And the stories that grown-ups told seemed so boring.

Across the cavernous room were the stairs leading to the lockers. As she snaked through the guests, Nat noticed Ewan heading down the stairs.

She smiled and hurried to the stairs. She thought Ewan was really cool.

She clomped down the stairs in her snowboarding boots. But Ewan wasn't there.

The door leading to the parking lot slammed shut.

Nat shrugged. She wasn't coming down here to hang with Ewan anyway.

Kevin's bag lay under the stairs leading to the locker room. It was a basic black backpack full of books and the trophy. Nat unzipped the main cargo pocket and reached in for the trophy.

"Huh?" Nat exclaimed. She pulled her hand out of the bag empty. She reached in again and dug around some more.

Again, her hand came out empty.

Nat lifted the bag and shook out its contents. A couple of school books fell out, along with a small tool kit for tweaking snowboards.

Dropping Kevin's bag, she grabbed Wall's and tore it open. No trophy. She did the same with Jamil's. Still no trophy.

"This is too weird," Nat muttered. Then she thought of Ewan. Would he have taken it? Would he have seen who did?

Nat dashed out the door into the parking lot. Cars splashed around in the slush and snow while skiers prepared to leave for the day. The lifts had already shut down. The only people on the slopes were those making their last run.

Nat jogged through the lot in search of Ewan. Cars were lined up to turn onto the highway leading out of the valley.

No luck. Ewan was gone.

She turned and bumped right into Bob Williams.

"Hey, kiddo, you better watch where you're going," Bob said as he caught Nat by the shoulders just before she fell.

"Sorry, Bob," Nat replied. "Have you seen Ewan McKendrick?"

Bob shook his head.

Nat went back inside.

"It's gone!" Kevin shouted. Kevin, Jamil, and Wall were crowded around the backpacks.

"Someone made a mess of them," Jamil observed. "They could've just stolen the bags."

"I made the mess," Nat interrupted. "I was looking for the trophy, but it's gone."

"Stolen?" Wall asked.

Nat nodded.

Jamil dug into his backpack. "At least he didn't steal my baseball." He held his baseball up to show his friends.

"How? Who?" Wall continued, ignoring Jamil.

"I think we've got ourselves a mystery," Jamil said.

4

"But who would steal it?" Kevin asked. "I don't get it." Kneeling, he shoved his books back in his bag. "Hey, what's this?" Kevin held up a piece of paper. "It says, 'You'll never find the statue, if you don't know how to look.'"

"What's that supposed to mean?" Jamil asked.

"I don't know, but I saw Ewan come down here just before me," Nat said. "Maybe he saw something."

"We should talk to him *now*," Jamil said forcefully. "We can't lose this trophy."

"Yeah. Otherwise, we won't have anything to give the winner of the competition," Wall added.

Nat leaned against the stairs and thought for a minute. "I don't get why anyone would steal it. It isn't like they can put it on their shelf and say they won it. Everyone will know."

"It doesn't make sense, but it happened," Kevin

replied. "There must be some reason. Maybe they think it's valuable."

"But it isn't," Wall added. "It cost us just a few bucks."

"That's true," Jamil admitted. "I knew something weird was going to happen."

"Stop being so superstitious," Nat said.

"I can't help it," Jamil defended himself. "This is a small town and all, but we ran into just about every suspect we ever had," Jamil explained. "And all of them could have seen the trophy."

"Yeah," Wall said excitedly. "Maybe one of them wants to get back at us for suspecting him."

"That's possible," Kevin replied. "But definitely a long shot."

Nat glanced out the door and saw that it was getting dark. "Okay. Here's the plan. Jamil and I will stop by Ewan's house. At least we know he was down here around the time the trophy was stolen. He could definitely have seen something."

"And he definitely could be playing with us for thinking he was behind the skate park mess," Jamil added.

"But was there enough time for him to steal it?" Nat asked. "He was out the door by the time I got down the stairs."

"Let's connect up online tonight," Kevin suggested.

They all agreed.

Jamil and Nat slipped out the lodge through the locker room exit, while Kevin and Wall went up the stairs back to the lodge's main room.

Across town, Nat and Jamil rang the doorbell of Ewan's grandparents' house. Ewan's parents traveled a lot, so he lived with his grandparents.

Flump. Flump. Flump. They heard loud footsteps coming to the door.

Nat and Jamil looked at each other with surprise.

"The Jolly Green Giant?" Jamil suggested.

Nat laughed.

The door swung open and the strangest person they have ever seen stood before them.

Nat was speechless.

Jamil started to laugh. "I didn't know Ewan lived with the clown family," Jamil blurted.

Nat whacked him.

The person at the door laughed. She was already smiling. In fact, her smile was so big, it covered half her face, because she was dressed up like a clown. "I'm Ewan's grandmother, Esther Dixon. Don't mind the costume. I'm a clown in tonight's fund-raising circus at the high school. You kids are coming, aren't you?"

"Uh, well, we weren't planning on it," Nat said.

Mrs. Dixon waved the kids inside. The house was an old Victorian and the shadowy hallway looked like it hadn't been changed since it was built. It was lined with dark wood and the tables were covered with all kinds of porcelain statues. "If you want to catch Ewan, you'll have to come to the fund-raiser. He'll be running one of the games. And he's got a surprise for everyone." She grabbed her purse and dug for her keys. "You must come. It's for a good cause—the student council."

"A surprise," Nat repeated. "We can't miss this." Just then she turned and the sleeve of her jacket knocked one of the statues off a table. "Oops."

Jamil reached out and caught it. He carefully set it back on the table.

"That was close," Nat gasped.

"We better leave," Mrs. Dixon said.

"Yeah, before Nat breaks something," Jamil cracked.

"Thanks," Nat replied.

They all stepped out of the house. Mrs. Dixon locked the door and went to her car. "Would you kids like a ride?"

"Yeah, that sounds great!" Nat answered. She and Jamil piled into the back seat.

As they drove up to the school, they saw groups of kids heading into the front doors. Other adults dressed as clowns were also there, ushering them in. Nat and Jamil thanked Mrs. Dixon for the ride and followed the crowds into the gymnasium.

"Do you think Ewan's surprise has anything to do with the stolen trophy?" Jamil asked.

Nat thought for a moment. "I don't see how, but we better check it out, just in case."

The circus performance didn't start for another hour. There were sideshows and games in the cafeteria to amuse people while they waited.

"Where should we start looking?" Jamil asked.

Nat grabbed his arm and pulled him along. "Not far."

Up ahead Ewan was sitting on a platform above a pool of water. People were throwing baseballs at a target next to the platform. When someone hit the target, Ewan dropped into the pool.

"I knew there was a reason I stuffed my baseball in my backpack this morning," Jamil said.

"Twenty-five cents a throw!" announced the worker handing out baseballs.

Jamil dug into his pocket and pulled out a quarter. "Here!"

The worker gave him a baseball.

Jamil threw. The crowd groaned at his miss.

"Let me try," Nat said. She handed over a quarter and took a baseball. She tossed the ball in the air a couple of times to get a feel for it. Then she wound up and threw.

Splash!

"Direct hit!" the worker shouted.

Ewan came burbling up out of the pool. "Thanks, Nat!" he laughed.

"Hey, Ewan!" Nat waved. "Got a sec?"

"Yeah. It's the principal's turn anyway." Ewan climbed out of the tank and grabbed a towel. "What's up?"

"I saw you in the lodge this afternoon about the time our trophy was stolen from Kevin's backpack," Nat started to explain.

Ewan held up his hands. "Not again. You suspect me of stealing the trophy? I thought you figured out last time that I'm not a thief."

"Well, uh, we did," Nat answered hesitantly. "But I saw you heading down the stairs to the locker room right before I discovered the trophy was missing."

"And we were wondering if you saw anything," Jamil said.

Ewan thought for a moment. A drop of water fell from the tip of his nose. He wiped his face with the towel. Then he shook his head. "No one. *Nada.*"

"Are you sure?" Nat pressed.

"Sorry," Ewan replied.

"Ladies and gentlemen, the greatest show in Hoke Valley is about to start in the auditorium!" someone announced to the crowd in the gym.

"I got to get out of this wet stuff," Ewan said. A puddle of water formed at his feet. He took off for the bathroom.

Nat shrugged. "So what do you want to do?"

"You thinking what I am?" Jamil asked.

Nat nodded and they headed for the auditorium.

Inside they found seats up front.

The first act was Cyrus McGowan, who owned Rumble Boards in town. He was billed as the Amazing Cyrus and came out in a black cape and top hat.

Nat and Jamil snickered. Cyrus's act was a little rough at the edges, especially when he dropped his cards. He did do a cool hoop trick and made a rabbit disappear.

The audience clapped enthusiastically.

"I like his card tricks," Jamil cracked.

"Yeah, fifty-two card pick up is one of the most original tricks I've ever seen." Nat laughed.

Next, Ewan shot out from behind the curtains on his inline skates.

"Excellent!" Nat shouted. Ewan was an awesome skater who could perform all kinds of tricks.

A couple of stage hands carried out a ramp, a three-foot-high wooden box, and a three-foot-high rail. Ewan circled the stage to pick up speed. Then he turned toward the rail and leaped high in the air. The grind plates on his skates clanged against the metal rail. He turned his skates so that the outside edges ground against the rail and pulled off a rad alien soul.

Barrett soars!

Snowboarder Barrett Christy

Although Barrett played many sports as a child growing up outside of Philadelphia, Pa., she didn't know about snowboarding until she moved to Lake Tahoe, Calif., when she was eighteen. After watching the snowboarders, she decided to try the sport herself. It took a while to feel comfortable on the board, but Barrett progressed faster than she ever had on skis. She soon moved to Crested Butte, Colo., and perfected her skills. Two years later, Barrett was off to Vail, Colo., where she began competing.

In 1994, Barrett began to compete professionally. The following year, she won the U.S. Xtreme Competition in Crested Butte. In 1997, Barrett won the Slopestyle event at the Sierra Free-Ride Competition, the Half Pipe and Big Air events at the U.S. Open, and the Slopestyle and Big Air events at the first winter X Games!

In 1998, Barrett made the Olympic team. She continues to live in Vail.

BARRETT'S SNOWBOARDING SAFETY TIPS

1. Know your limits.
2. Always visualize what you're going to do— go through the motions in your head from takeoff to landing.
3. Don't be scared to wear a helmet.
4. Wear equipment that fits your size and ability level.

GRABBING MUTE, SPINNING THROUGH THE AIR

Barrett at age 10

Age: 27

Most memorable competition: The first U.S. Xtreme competition in Crested Butte, Colo., 1995, because it snowed three feet before my event and the three days felt more like free-riding than anything else.

Favorite athlete: John Elway for his endurance and his ability to withstand beatings on the field.

Favorite snowboard: Gnu snowboards by Mervin Manufacturing.

What I like best about my sport: The ability to express individual style—everyone has their own. But free-riding on the mountains with real snow is still the heart and soul of it.

Favorite thing to do on a Saturday: Wake up early, go to yoga class, and take my time as I eat a big breakfast and enjoy various activities like tennis, mountain biking, and swimming.

Favorite pig-out food: Cheese steak sandwiches—but only from Philly!

He came off the rail in one fluid motion, kicked his blades a couple of times to pick up speed, he rolled up the ramp, and hucked a Lu Kang. His right leg straightened as he brought his left skate to his rear and grabbed the toe.

Nat glanced around and saw people in the audience with their jaws hanging open. Ewan was *that* good.

Landing with the grace of a swan, he kicked his skates a couple of times and headed straight for the box. Like a pogo stick, he bounced up to the edge, crossed his skates and ground out a stylin' unity.

He popped off the box and landed with a loud bang that echoed through the auditorium. He kicked one skate and tucked into a fishbrain that took him straight for the edge of the stage.

People in the first row ducked as Ewan flew off the stage. He turned his fishbrain into a flying fish.

"I've never seen that before," Jamil gasped.

Nat grinned. She was the first of the crew to appreciate inline skating, but now even Jamil, a skateboard freak, was into it.

"This guy is huge!" Jamil said.

Ewan skated up the aisle, turned and hauled back toward the stage. The stagehands had placed a ramp about ten feet from the stage. Ewan aimed right for it. He came up the ramp, sailed high into the air, and pulled off an awesome McTwist. He spun 540 degrees like a top and landed on center stage.

Everyone was on their feet, clapping.

Ewan turned and bowed. Then he skated off stage.

The audience screamed for more, but circus music was cranked up. It was time for the parade.

People in costumes started marching down the aisles. There were clowns as well as people dressed as horses, elephants, and half a dozen other animals.

"Let's jet," Nat whispered to Jamil.

Jamil nodded. They slipped out the side door.

6

Later that evening Nat sat at her desk in the bedroom she shared with her sister. As she waited for her computer to boot up, she took the note the X-crew found in Kevin's backpack out of her pocket. She spread the paper on the desk.

Across the room, Ella laid on her bed, reading her Thompson Triplets book. "Nat, you've got to listen to this."

"I'm busy," Nat replied. She clicked to load her Internet program.

"No, really. This is cool. You'll like it since you're such a big detective," Ella continued.

"I'm busy," Nat repeated.

"But this Thompson Triplets story is just the kind of thing you guys solve," Ella argued.

"I'm not interested. I've got my own mystery to work on," Nat said.

Ella stared at her sister for a moment. Then she began reading silently.

Nat entered the Xtreme chatroom on the Hoke Valley Network.

Three people were lingering in the chatroom. Their online tags told her they were her friends: WallIt, Kevlar, and JamMan.

Nat typed: *Did Jamil tell you about Ewan?*

Kevlar: *Yeah. But it doesn't help, does it?*

WallIt: *Nope. We're stuck.*

Nat glanced down at the note again. Then it hit her. The note was handwritten. She typed furiously.

Wait, guys. Remember the note was handwritten. We can compare suspects' handwriting to the note. All we have to do is get some samples.

WallIt: *Smart, but who are our suspects?*

JamMan: *We have none.*

Kevlar: *Yes, we do. Remember who was around when we pulled out the trophy?*

JamMan: *About half the town.*

Kevlar: *Yeah, but also all our old suspects. Like Jamil said earlier, what if one of them wanted to get back at us? It would be the perfect way.*

NatSk8: *You know I saw Bob Williams at the lodge around the time the trophy was stolen as well. He was also at the bookstore when we pulled the trophy out.*

JamMan: *What does the note say again?*

NatSk8: *"You'll never find the statue, if you don't know how to look."*

WallIt: *It's strange that the note says "how to look" instead of "where to look". It's like we have to have a special way of going about solving our mystery. I don't get it.*

Kevlar: *Let's stick to what we do get. "How" we can search is by looking at the handwriting. And that means getting samples from at least Bob and Ewan.*

NatSk8: *We should also get samples from Mitch, Mark, Phil, Ian, and Mr. Mack since we ran into all of them at the store. Any one of them could have snuck into the lodge while we were riding.*

WallIt: *Good point, but Ewan and Bob seem more likely. Should we bother with the others?*

Kevlar: *Might as well. I'll get samples from Mitch and Mark. They're in my science class.*

JamMan: *Ian's in my gym class, and a sample of Bob's writing will be on his season pass application in my dad's office. I can get that too.*

NatSk8: *I know I've got a sample of Ewan's writing somewhere in my room since he was on the skate park committee with me. Phil is going to be tough, but I might find something in the Bear Claw offices. I'll check there.*

WallIt: *I guess that leaves me Mr. Mack. Thanks a lot, guys.*

NatSk8: *Good hunting. Let's meet at the pipe tomorrow afternoon.*

They all signed off and headed for the sack. Tomorrow was going to be a big day.

Nat sat at her desk and sorted through her drawers. She wanted to check Ewan's handwriting right away and she had a sample of it somewhere in her Skate Park Committee folder.

"What are you looking for?" Ella asked. Ella sat up and tried to see what Nat was doing.

Nat ignored her until she had looked through every drawer. "Have you seen my skate park files?"

Ella closed her book and pulled the covers up. "Look

on the top shelf."

Nat stood on her chair and reached for a stack of papers on the top of her bookshelf. She sorted through them until she came to a folder marked "Skate Park Committee." Inside were notes, fund-raising letters, and all the other material the committee had generated. Nat had saved everything.

"Here it is." Nat slid out a draft of a petition that Ewan had written by hand a few months earlier. She laid it beside the note from Kevin's backpack.

The handwriting on the two pieces of paper didn't match. The "l's" and "t's" slanted in the opposite direction, while the "a's" and "n's" were looped very differently.

Nat sighed. She was relieved that Ewan's writing didn't match, but she was also disappointed that the mystery couldn't be solved so quickly. She wanted that trophy back as soon as possible.

Nat put Ewan's paper back in the folder and replaced the papers on the top shelf. Then she stuck the note in the front pocket of her backpack. She knew she'd need it the next day to compare it to the others' samples.

As Nat climbed into bed, she looked across the room at her sister. Ella had fallen asleep. She thought about what her dad had said earlier in the day. Maybe she *had* been too hard on Ella. She did help her find the folder just now. But Ella was such a pain, especially around other people.

Hours before school started the next morning, Jamil was up and out of the house. In the dark he crossed the large parking lot from his family's condo to the resort's main lodge. The light of his flashlight bobbed in front of him.

Jamil wanted to get to his dad's office before his dad did. And that meant getting up at five AM. In the winter his dad was usually in his office by six-thirty. The lifts opened at eight and there was always a lot to do before then.

The basement office was small and cramped. Not the kind of office one would think the manager of a large resort would have, but Jamil's dad preferred to spend his days on the mountain, not in the office.

Jamil had to sort his way through all kinds of equipment—skis, snowboards, a lift chair tipped on its side. His dad's file cabinet was behind the desk. The second drawer down was marked "Season Passes." Jamil slid open the drawer and immediately went to the back where the "W's" began. Bob Williams's form was slipped between Whittemore and Wilson. Jamil pulled it out and examined it.

Suddenly, Jamil heard footsteps. He closed the file cabinet drawer and hurried from his dad's office. As he turned the corner to go out the locker room exit, he ran smack into his dad.

"Jamil!" Mr. Smith said with surprise.

Jamil quickly hid Bob Williams's application behind his back. "Uh, morning, Dad. How are you?"

Mr. Smith looked at his son suspiciously. Then he held out his hand. "Give it over."

"What? I don't have anything," Jamil protested.

"What are you hiding behind your back?"

Busted. Reluctantly, Jamil showed his dad Bob's application.

"What are you doing with this?" Mr. Smith asked angrily. "You're not supposed to be looking at these, let alone stealing one."

"I'm sorry, Dad, but I have an explanation," Jamil stammered. "I've got to compare Bob's handwriting to a note left by the person who stole the trophy. I was going to return it."

Mr. Smith nodded. He remembered Jamil telling him the night before about the trophy being stolen. "I can sympathize with you wanting to get the trophy back. I also feel a little bit responsible since it was stolen at the lodge, but I can't let you take personal information from the files. It's unethical."

Jamil hung his head.

"Come back this afternoon with the writing sample and I'll compare it with Bob's writing," Mr. Smith finally said.

"Thanks, Dad!" Jamil replied.

"Now, go home and get ready for school. I've got some repairs to do on the main lift," Mr. Smith said.

An hour later across town, Nat sat down to breakfast with her family. She mixed granola and dried fruit into her yogurt. Her father poured cups of coffee for himself and her mother while her mother finished buttering some toast. Ella finished up her oatmeal and then moved onto some cereal, toast, and frozen blueberries. Ella liked her blueberries frozen, just like she liked her peas.

"How about this?" Mr. Whittemore said, as he scratched a couple of words onto a piece of paper. He was helping Ella out on a school assignment. She had to come up with as many words as possible from the letters in her name.

Ella glanced over. "Hello, Meteor, Motel, Hotel, Write. I got those already, Dad." She showed him her list. "But I can't seem to come up with a word or phrase that uses all of the letters."

"How about this?" Mr. Whittemore answered, as he wrote *Ethel Mowertail*.

"What's that?" Ella said impatiently.

"It's a name," Mr. Whittemore explained. "Ethel is the first name and Mowertail is the second."

"Never heard of it," Ella replied. "Get serious, Dad."

"When's this assignment due?" Mrs. Whittemore asked as she poured herself another cup of coffee.

"Yesterday," Nat commented.

Ella stuck her tongue out.

"I think this is something Ella should work on herself, Jake," Mrs. Whittemore said. Then she turned to Nat. "So what's up with your club?"

"Major problem. Our trophy was stolen," Nat said.

"What?" Mrs. Whittemore replied.

Nat nodded. Then she explained how someone stole it and left a note in Kevin's backpack.

"Hey! That sounds just like what happened in my Thompson Triplets mystery," Ella piped up.

"Yeah, right," Nat said sarcastically. Nat brought her dishes to the sink and rinsed them off.

Ella worked on her homework. "I just don't understand why the competition is limited to only junior high kids."

"It's not," Nat replied as she snagged her parka. "High school kids can compete, too."

"Mom!" Ella whined. "It's not fair. My friends should be able to compete, too."

"Why don't you have your own competition?" Mr. Whittemore suggested.

Ella brightened. "Yeah! I could have my own club."

"Dad! I can't believe you told her to copy me," Nat said. She grabbed her backpack.

"You're not in charge of everything," Mrs.

Whittemore said. "If you won't include her, she can certainly do it on her own."

"You shouldn't be so dismissive of Ella," Mr. Whittemore added.

"Thanks," Nat replied, as she slammed the door behind her. She couldn't believe how hard her parents were coming down on her, especially when she had a competition to organize *and* a stolen trophy to find.

8

Later that morning, Kevin slipped into science class and scanned the room for Mitch and Mark. They were sitting in the last row of desks. There was an empty desk beside Mark, and Kevin made for it.

"Hey, Kev," Mitch said. "What are you lost or something?"

"Yeah. Aren't you a first row kind of guy?" Mark added. He was slumped in his chair with his cap turned backwards on his head.

"I need a new perspective," Kevin answered and sat down. He wasn't sure yet how he was going to pull this off, but he figured he'd think of something by the end of the class.

Just then, the buzz of the public address system being turned on filled the room. Everyone in the class looked up at the speaker like they could see who was talking.

"Attention, we have a short announcement," the principal said.

"Next Saturday, the Hoke Valley Middle School Snowboarding Club is sponsoring a half pipe competition. Everyone is welcome to enter. Sign up outside the office," Nat said. "There will be prizes and a trophy for the winner."

The public address system clicked off.

A murmur of excitement rippled through the classroom.

"Okay, everyone," Mr. Clary spoke loudly. "We have a lot of work to do today." He started lecturing about the science experiment they were going to do that day.

That's when Kevin got the idea that he could get a writing sample then. Everyone had to take notes on the experiment.

Kevin managed to get both Mitch and Mark in his group.

"We'll all take notes," Kevin said. "Mr. Clary likes it when you turn in a lot of data."

"You would know," Mitch replied. "You're the 'A' student."

Mark and Mitch each tore a sheet of paper out of their notebooks. Kevin conducted the experiment and the three of them took notes. At the end of class, Kevin brought the results to the front of the class, but he didn't hand in all of the papers. Instead, he slipped Mitch and Mark's into his pocket and handed in just his own. Mr. Clary really needed only one set of notes, not three.

The bell rang.

"Lunch!" someone shouted.

Kevin headed for his locker, which was right next to Nat's. When he got there, he noticed an envelope sticking out of Nat's locker door. He slid it partially out and saw Nat's name written on it.

Nat had lunch now, too, so Kevin grabbed the envelope and brought it to the cafeteria.

Kevin spotted Nat and Wall at the far end of the lunchroom at their usual table.

"Found this sticking out of your locker," Kevin said, as he tossed the envelope on her tray.

"You know stealing someone's mail is a federal offense." Nat tore open the envelope.

"Very funny," Kevin replied. "What's in it?"

Nat pulled out a piece of paper with a short sentence on it. "You must know the story to find the statue."

"What's that supposed to mean?" Wall asked.

"Got me," Kevin replied.

Nat pulled out the first note and laid it beside the new one. "Hey! This new one has a different handwriting than the first."

"Could there be two thieves?" Wall exclaimed.

9

Nat, Jamil, Kevin, and Wall sat on the floor outside Mr. Smith's office and waited for him to get off the phone.

Nat sniffed. "What's that smell?"

"French fries and soggy carpet," Jamil answered. "My dad loves fries and the carpet is always wet from the snow people track in. Sometimes at night he turns on fans to dry the rugs out."

"Is he really going to help us?" Wall asked.

"Sure. Why not? He said he would," Jamil replied.

Mr. Smith's office door swung open. "Hey! I didn't realize it took all of you to check out this handwriting."

Nat stood. "We're all just anxious to find the trophy," she explained.

Everyone followed Mr. Smith into the office.

"Sorry for the mess," Mr. Smith said, as he stepped over a broken snowboard. He sat behind his desk and popped a fry dripping with ketchup in his mouth.

Nat pulled out the two notes and handed them over. "Could you check these against Bob's application?" The fries were making her hungry.

Mr. Smith laid the notes and the application flat on his desk. He picked up one and read it aloud. "You must know the story to find the statue." Then he picked up the other. "You'll never find the statue, if you don't know how to look." He looked up at the crew. "This is a tough puzzle."

"But do either of the notes match Bob's handwriting?" Jamil pressed.

"They don't match," he replied without looking at the notes again.

"But you hardly looked," Jamil protested.

"It's obvious. Bob doesn't write like this," Mr. Smith replied.

"Can we look?" Kevin asked.

"Well . . ." Mr. Smith considered the request. "I'd like to, but I just don't feel comfortable sharing private information publicly. What if Bob finds out? I know he'd blow his top." He ate another french fry.

Nat sighed and turned to her friends. "I guess that's it."

"Jamil, don't forget you said you would tune some rental boards," Mr. Smith said.

"I'm on my way," Jamil said.

The crew exited Mr. Smith's office.

In the hallway, Jamil suggested, "You guys can ride if you want while I'm tuning the boards."

"First, I need some french fries," Nat said. "Your dad was driving me crazy."

"Yeah, I was hoping he'd offer us some," Wall added. They laughed.

Jamil took his friends to the kitchen where he served up some fries, and they headed to the rental shop.

On the way, Kevin said, "Let's talk about what we have so far and then we can ride."

The rental shop was down the hall from Mr. Smith's office. A stack of snowboards stood behind the counter waiting to be tuned.

It was a weekday, so the rental store was empty, except for one clerk.

"Hi, Deb."

"Hey, Jamil. Your dad said you'd be in to work on boards," Deb replied. She was tall and thin with short brown hair. She was taking a year off from college to spend the winter on the mountain.

"These are my friends Nat, Kevin, and Wall," Jamil said, waving to the crew.

"Hi," Deb said.

The gang said hi and followed Jamil behind the counter.

As she watched Jamil lock the first board into the clamp, Nat swished a fry in a pool of ketchup. "I don't get this second note. What does it mean when it says we have to know the story? What story?"

Kevin shook his head. "You got me." He stuffed four fries in his mouth at once.

Jamil picked up a Carborundum stone and worked the base edge from the tip to the tail using smooth, even strokes. The edge on this board was worn pretty badly and had nicks all over the place. Jamil had his work cut out for him.

Wall watched Jamil work for a minute. "Story . . . My dad is always telling me not to tell him a story, and he means don't lie. What if this note is referring to someone lying to us? Maybe we have to know who is lying to us."

"You're the man," Jamil said. "That's good." He dragged the stone along the edge and smoothed the nicks and burrs.

Wall sat back and grinned.

"Okay, so who is lying to us?" Nat asked.

"Or who is *going* to lie to us?" Kevin asked. "We haven't talked to everyone we planned to."

"That's true," Jamil said. "I've still got to get a writing sample from Ian." Jamil picked up an 8-inch mill file and worked on a zero-degree base edge.

"And I can't even imagine how I'm going to get one from Mr. Mack," Wall said sadly.

"And I've got to look for one from Phil Speck," Nat added.

"But let's think about who we've talked to so far," Kevin said. "Nat and Jamil interviewed Ewan."

"And we just interviewed Jamil's dad," Wall said.

Jamil unclamped the first board and put it on the rack. "Wait a sec. Didn't my dad act weird a few minutes ago?"

"How so?" Kevin asked.

"Well, he hardly looked at the writing. It was like he already knew Bob wasn't the culprit, so he didn't have to look at the samples," Jamil explained. He clamped the next board onto the work table. This board had a small gouge in its base. Jamil reached over and grabbed a P-tex candle.

"Now, you're being paranoid," Wall said. "He said it was really obvious."

"Well, why didn't he show us?" Nat asked.

Jamil lit the candle and dripped the P-tex into the gouge a little bit at a time. When it was filled, he blew out the candle and grabbed a steel scraper. He shaved away the excess P-tex.

"It was a privacy issue," Wall replied, taking Mr. Smith's side.

"Something smell's fishy," Kevin said.

"I'll try talking to my dad tonight and see if I can trip him up," Jamil volunteered. He picked up a sandpaper block and started to texture the base. He passed the block from tip to tail with a 100-grit paper and a 120-grit paper. Then he polished the base with an abrasive pad.

"That's a good start," Kevin replied. "But we've got to continue investigating our other leads. We need to follow up on Ian and Phil." Suddenly Kevin slapped his forehead. "And I almost forgot." He pulled a couple of pieces of paper out of his pocket. "Here are Mark and Mitch's writing samples."

They laid the samples next to the notes on the table.

"There you guys are. I've been looking all over for you," Ella said as she entered the shop. "What're you doing?"

"We're busy," Nat said without looking up.

Ella sat leaned against the front of the counter. "What're those?" She pointed at the papers on the work table.

"No match," Kevin sighed. He crumpled up Mark and Mitch's samples and tossed them in the garbage.

Nat glanced at her sister.

Ella smiled. "I'm working on my half pipe competition. I was wondering how you guys reserved a date."

"We've got a mystery to solve," Nat said impatiently. "We don't have time to hold your hand." Nat gestured at the notes on the table. "These notes were left by the thief and we've got to figure out what they mean."

"Talk to my dad," Jamil said to Ella. "He'll put you in the calendar."

"Thanks, Jamil." Ella leaned over and looked more closely at the notes. "What kind of notes are these? The mystery I'm reading had notes from a thief, too." She took a few seconds to read the notes. Then she gasped. "These notes are the same as in the Thompson Triplets book!"

"Yeah, right." Nat didn't believe her. "You're not going to get our attention that way."

"No, really. They are," Ella protested.

"Let's see," Nat said holding her hand out.

"The book's at home, but I swear it," Ella insisted.

Kevin turned to his friends. "If Ella is right, then we might have solved the mystery. The book could be the story the thief is referring to!"

"And that could be what he means by 'how to look' instead of 'where to look,'" Jamil added.

"Now we're getting somewhere," Wall said, rubbing his hands together. "So how does the story end, Ella?"

Ella shrugged. "Haven't finished it yet."

"Let's get it," Nat said. "We can jump right to the end."

"No way!" Ella shot back. "You're not reading my book. I'll tell you what the end says when I'm done with it."

Nat rolled her eyes. "I'm sure the bookstore has a copy of it."

Ella smiled smugly. "No it doesn't. I have the only copy."

"Are you almost finished?" Kevin asked.

Ella nodded. She was enjoying the attention. "I can finish it tonight. But only if you include kids my age in your competition."

"No way!" Nat shouted. "You're not going to hold us hostage." She pointed a finger at her sister. "Dad'll make you show me."

"Will not," Ella replied.

"Will too."

Kevin held up his hands. "Okay, you two. You've been on a collision course for days."

Nat slumped her shoulders. Her brow was knit tightly.

Ella stood opposite her with her arms tightly crossed. Neither was going to budge.

"We can wait until Ella finishes the book tonight," Kevin conceded.

"And I don't see why we can't let grammar school kids in the comp too," Wall said. "I say, the more the merrier."

"Me, too," Jamil confirmed.

Nat didn't answer, but she did give a slight nod.

Kevin breathed a sigh of relief. "Then it's settled."

Ella jumped up. "I'm going to go finish the book." She ran out of the lodge.

"Now I don't have to track down Mr. Mack's handwriting," Wall said with relief.

10

"I say we don't waste any time waiting for Ella," Nat suddenly said. "Let's finish investigating the handwriting. We might be able to solve this mystery without my little sister's help."

"Give her a chance, Nat," Kevin replied. "What's it matter if she helps?"

"She's a pain. She wouldn't even let us look at her book," Nat explained.

"She just wants to be a part of things," Jamil argued. "If you didn't exclude her so much, we probably wouldn't be in this situation."

Nat pulled on her parka. "Well, I'm going to the Bear Claw offices and then to Ian's barn. Anyone want to come?"

Jamil shook his head. "I've still got to wax this one and then I've got five more boards to tune."

Kevin shook his head. "I'm going to ride. I can wait one more day for Ella."

Wall stared for a moment at Nat. Then he looked down at his feet. "I'm going to hang, too."

"Fine," Nat said curtly. She started to walk out of the rental shop when she suddenly stopped. "Wait a second! What if Ella is behind all this to get some attention?"

"You've got to be kidding," Jamil replied.

"Nat's got a point," Wall suggested. "She's been bugging us to be a part of the comp."

"And now she's in," Nat said. "See, I told you."

"Do you really think she could be that sneaky?" Kevin asked skeptically.

"She is Nat's sister, isn't she?" Jamil answered.

They all laughed.

"You've got a point there," Kevin replied with a laugh. "Nat is pretty devious so it only makes sense that her sister would be, too."

"Thanks guys," Nat cracked. "But seriously, she saw the trophy and she heard our plans. She could easily have stolen it and left the note. Who else is reading the book?"

"Ella did trap herself when she said she has the only copy," Wall admitted. "She definitely had a motive to steal the trophy, and she had the opportunity to steal it while we were riding."

"But what about the handwriting?" Kevin reminded everyone. "The notes can't be in her handwriting. She's just a kid."

"Yeah, you're right," Nat admitted. "Ella likes to dot

her *i*'s with big circles. These notes were definitely written by someone else."

"Maybe we have to wait for Ella to make the next move," Kevin suggested. "Either she tells us how the mystery ends and we solve our mystery, or she returns the trophy. It's that simple."

Nat nodded. "I hate to admit it, but you're right, Kev. I just wish we could beat her at her own game."

Finally, Wall shrugged. "Nat, why don't you come for a ride with us. You can check out Phil and Ewan's handwriting later."

"Oh, all right," Nat replied.

Nat, Wall, and Kevin grabbed their snowboards from their lockers, while Jamil finished his tuning work in the rental shop. They had about an hour of light left, so they hurried to the lift.

"And I thought I wasn't going to ride today," Nat said happily as they rode up the chair lift.

"Winter's too short not to ride every day," Wall replied.

A wind kicked snow up into little tornadoes below them. The chairlift ran up a clear cut between a thick forest of pines. Long, late-afternoon shadows darkened the mountain. As the kids sat quietly and rode the lift, an occasional crack of a branch breaking under the weight of snow echoed around them.

Nat tightened the red scarf around her neck. She felt her neck and shoulders tighten. She tried to relax them because she knew that getting tense would only make her colder. Next, she concentrated on tightening and then relaxing each of her muscles. Starting with her toes and moving up her body, she worked at keeping herself loose—and warm.

The chair came up over a crest and the lift exit came into sight. It was a high, steep mound covered in snow.

Nat, Wall, and Kevin lifted the noses of their boards and pushed the safety gate up over their heads. They each turned sideways so they could come off the chair and ride down the steep slope easily.

When it was time, they pushed off the chair. Nat set her rear foot on her stomp pad and went to the left. Kevin did the same and went to the right. And Wall stomped and went straight ahead, but the edge of his board caught on some thick, crusty crud. It pulled him along so that he couldn't stop. This wasn't good, because he was heading straight for a huge metal chairlift pole.

"Agh!" Wall threw himself into a mound of snow.

Clap! Clap! Clap! Nat stood to the side, applauding Wall's bonk.

Wall lifted his head and smiled. "Pretty good, huh?" He rolled over on his hands and knees and pushed himself up. Then he skated over to the top of the slope.

"Follow the leader again?" Kevin asked.

"I'm tired of that game," Nat said. "Let's just ride and get the kinks out."

Wall sat to strap his back foot on. "It just occurred to me. The handwriting in that second note is familiar."

"Your crash must have knocked some sense into you," Kevin cracked.

"Exactly," Wall deadpanned. "And what I came up with is that the second note was written by a left-hander."

"Explain," Kevin prompted.

"Jamil is left-handed. Jamil's handwriting is angled in the same way as the second note. So the second note must be written by someone who is left-handed." Wall pushed himself up to his feet.

"So you're saying Jamil could have written the second note?" Nat asked.

"No, that's not what I mean," Wall said, trying to explain. "I just want to point out that the second note writer is left-handed and the first is right-handed."

"This is terrific!" Nat said excitedly. "But what can we do with it?"

Wall shrugged. "Nothing, I guess. But it's one more piece of the puzzle. Maybe it'll help somewhere down the line."

"Then I'm going to ride," Kevin said. He turned down the fall line and took the double black diamond trail.

"Go speed racer!" Nat shouted after him. Then she started down the hill.

Wall went the opposite way and took a slope that had two awesome jumps.

Nat headed straight for the steep mogul field that was called Freight Train. It was like a parking lot of VW Beetles buried in three feet of snow and tilted at a 30-degree angle.

To most, this would be a recipe for ending up in the hospital. For Nat, this was *fun!*

She began by turning in the deep troughs of the moguls, coming around each one like she was doing the do-si-do at a square dance.

The fall line on the slope took a steep turn, so Nat changed her focus from straight down the hill to a tree across the mogul field. She traversed across the slope and around the massive humps to the tree. Throwing her uphill shoulder downhill, she pointed her head toward where she wanted to go and made a smooth turn. It's amazing how the body always follows the head, Nat thought.

The rear of her board slipped a little. She dug her edge in more sharply and got it easily back under control.

Gaining confidence, Nat decided to ride down the fall line. She approached the first bump slowly and squared her shoulders over the board. Like shock absorbers, her knees sucked up the bumps. Then she extended them as she came over the mogul and dropped into the trough. Powder sprayed into the air.

After the next two moguls, Nat fell into a rhythm. Her head floated level, while her lower body bounced like a spring over the bumps.

The cold air felt tight in her lungs, but made her body feel alive. She surged down the steep run. As she came into the late afternoon shadows, it became difficult to judge the terrain. The distance between the moguls was hard to judge and the depth was lost in the receding light. Nat had to trust her rhythm and be aggressive. She started making jump turns at the tops of the moguls, not waiting for the safety of the trough.

She finally boarded out of Freight Train and in minutes was back at the lodge. She glanced around for her friends, but they weren't down yet. As she caught her breath, she thought about her sister holding all of the cards. She couldn't do anything without Ella. Nat didn't like this. And that's when Nat had a brainstorm.

"Maybe I don't have to wait for Ella," Nat thought out loud. She quickly grabbed her board and carried it into the lodge where she put it in her locker. She left a note for Kevin and Wall before running out the door and running down the street away from Hoke Valley Ski Resort.

11

Nat and her family lived in an apartment above the Book Worm. The brick two-story building was located on a side street off the Market Place, an area closed off to vehicles.

As she turned down her street, she saw her mother coming out of the store. She really didn't want to stop and talk with her so she tried to duck into the doorway that led up to their apartment.

"Natalie!"

"Ugh," Nat groaned.

"Wait!" her mother called. Mrs. Whittemore was a tall, thin woman who wore thick glasses and rarely dressed appropriately for the cold. She was wearing a sweater and no gloves. As she spoke, she wrapped her arms around herself to keep warm. "Could you make the salad? I'm on my way to get a couple of roasted chickens from Reiner's Deli."

Nat slumped against the doorsill. "Do I have to? Couldn't Ella do it?"

"No." Mrs. Whittemore hurried down the street. Reiner's Deli was about to close.

Nat stomped up the flight of stairs to the apartment. Inside, she hung her jacket on a hook and kicked off her boots. "Ella?" she called cautiously.

No answer.

Nat went down the hall and glanced in the bathroom.

Empty.

Nat then turned to the bedroom she shared with her sister. It was empty, too.

Nat entered and went straight to Ella's bed. The blankets were wadded up in a ball and the top sheet was shoved all the way to the foot of the bed. The pillow hung off the side.

Nat grimaced. She hated messes. She made her bed and picked up her dirty clothes every morning. She was a real neatnik. Ignoring her sister's mess, she knelt under the bed to search for the trophy.

It was dark underneath the bed and Nat had to reach into the darkness without being able to see. As she blindly probed with her hand, she felt something soft and furry.

Nat knew exactly what she was holding. Pulling it out only confirmed it. Nat had found her special teddy bear, which had been lost for two weeks. Ella had hidden it under her bed.

Steamed, Nat put Teddy on her pillow and went into

the kitchen. She dug around for the flashlight under the sink.

"Here it is," she said, determined to get a better look under Ella's bed. "Now, let's see what else she's hiding." Nat hurried down the hall. She was certain she'd find the statue now that she knew Ella was a thief.

Nat turned the flashlight on. She swept its light under the bed, but found nothing else important. Just some dirty old socks, a book, and a deck of cards. Nat stood up and went to Ella's dresser. She searched through the drawers and found nothing but clothes. Next, she moved on to Ella's desk. It was another mess. Nat didn't know how Ella could do homework at it. Then she remembered that Ella did her homework on her bed. Nat sorted through the pile of junk and rattled through the drawers, but again found nothing.

"Where else?" Nat asked herself as she stood in the middle of the room. "Where could that trophy be?"

Nat heard the door to the apartment slam. She shoved the flashlight under her bed and hurried down the hall.

Mrs. Whittemore stood at the kitchen counter. "Where's the salad?" she asked.

Nat blushed. "I was just about to make it," Nat stammered.

Mrs. Whittemore narrowed her eyes and stared at her daughter. But she said nothing.

Nat prepared the salad, while Mrs. Whittemore cut the chicken into pieces.

After supper, Nat sat at the kitchen table doing homework. Her legs swung under her chair as she worked on a knotty math problem. She wished Kevin was there. He was a whiz at math, while her best subjects were English, French, and history.

Suddenly, a scream came from down the hall. "Mom! Natalie's been touching my stuff!"

Nat buried her head in her books.

Mr. Whittemore came out of the living room with a book in his hand. "Ella, please don't shout!" he shouted down the hall.

Ella stormed out of the bedroom. "But Dad," she whined, "Nat's been on my side of the room."

Mr. Whittemore gave Nat a stern look. "Is this true?"

"But she stole my teddy," Nat protested.

Mr. Whittemore held up his hand like a traffic cop. "I don't want to hear it from either of you. You two have to learn to get along. You're sisters. Now I want you both to apologize to each other."

"Sorry," Ella said quickly.

Nat did the same.

"I just wish you two could learn to appreciate each other," Mr. Whittemore said.

Ella went back to their bedroom.

Mr. Whittemore sat at the kitchen table. "Nat, you're the oldest. You should set a better example for your sister."

"I know, Dad," Nat reluctantly admitted. She knew it

was always better not to argue with the 'rents. She would never win.

"I'd hate to see you two grow up fighting," Mr. Whittemore explained. "My sister and I did that, and for a long time we hardly talked."

Nat nodded, but inside she groaned. Parents just don't understand.

12

"Where could she have hidden it?" Nat asked her friends, as they sat in the hallway just before school started the next day. It was too cold to wait for the bell outside, so students were allowed to wait in the main hall.

"Maybe we're wrong," Kevin suggested. "Maybe Ella didn't steal the trophy. We don't have any hard evidence to prove she did."

"We all admitted that she couldn't have written the notes," Wall reminded everyone.

"Did she finish the book?" Jamil asked Nat.

Nat shrugged. "I don't know. We weren't talking to each other after our fight last night."

"Great," Kevin said with disgust. He slapped his gloves against the linoleum floor. "Just when we need your sister's help the most, you decide to get in a fight with her. You've got to be nicer to Ella."

"Especially when we need something from her," Jamil added.

"I'm sorry, but if she was your sister, you'd do the same," Nat insisted. She wadded her jacket behind her back to make a pillow against the cinderblock wall.

"Ella's not that bad," Kevin replied.

"I think she's funny," Jamil said. "You just don't give her a chance."

Nat stared at the fluorescent lights hanging from the ceiling. She couldn't believe her friends were turning against her. Or were they? Maybe they have a point, she thought. They're pretty much saying the same thing her dad said before. Can they all be wrong?

"Okay, I'll admit I wasn't the most tactful," Nat finally said. "But it's not going to do us any good to whine over spilled milk. Let's continue our search for the person who wrote the notes. If Ella helps us, great. If she doesn't, then we still have to find the trophy."

"Let's get back to the basics," Kevin said. Kevin fanned himself with a school book. With all the kids crowded into the hall and the heat cranked up, it felt like a sauna. "After school we'll check out Phil Speck's handwriting at the Bear Claw offices."

"That means I'm back to getting a writing sample from Mr. Mack," Wall groaned.

"Then we'll head over to Ian's barn and get a sample from him," Kevin said.

"That's if we don't see Ian at school today," Jamil replied, as he peeled off his sweater.

63

"We won't," Wall said. "He's on a band trip to Central City Opera today. He won't be back until this afternoon."

"I forgot about the trip," Jamil said. "I wish I was on that trip."

"Yeah, anything is better than school," Wall added.

Just then the bell rang.

Everyone jumped up to avoid being trampled by the hordes.

The plow had piled snow right up to the door of the building that held the Bear Claw offices.

"This is great," Wall said as he saw the snow piled about four feet high against the door.

"Start digging," Kevin said, as he scampered up the mound.

Jamil disappeared around the building and came back with a shovel. "Hey, I found a shovel!"

"Good. Now you can shovel the snow," Nat said.

"Wait a sec. I found the shovel so I shouldn't have to shovel," Jamil protested. "I should get some credit for saving us from digging with our hands."

"Whoever found it shovels with it," Wall cracked.

Jamil started to shovel. In a matter of minutes the door was clear. The crew bounded up the stairs.

Nat unlocked the door to the offices. "I think it's over here." She opened a drawer to a tall file cabinet in the corner. "There should be a race course route that Phil drew and made notes on." She quickly flipped through files.

Kevin, Wall, and Jamil found seats around the room to wait.

"Here it is!" Nat said triumphantly. She laid the paper on a table and turned on the desk lamp. Then she placed the two notes next to Phil's handwriting sample.

Everyone crowded around.

"The *L*s on the first note match Phil's," Kevin said.

"Really?" Jamil said excitedly. "Maybe we got this mystery cracked."

"Not so fast," Wall cut in. "The *N*s, *G*s, and *A*s are not even close."

"And just about every other letter," Nat complained. She shoved Phil's writing sample back in the folder and closed the file drawer.

"Maybe Ian's in his barn," Jamil said as they left the Bear Claw offices. Ian had turned the abandoned barn on his family's property into a rockin' indoor half pipe.

"But it's not heated," Nat replied.

"And hanging out at the snowboarding pipe is any different?" Jamil countered. They were crunching through the snow to the edge of town toward Ian's house.

Nat laughed. "I guess you're right."

Ian's yard was quiet. There were no cars in the driveway and no music blaring from the barn.

Wall waded through the snow to the barn and pushed open the door. When he stepped in, it was like entering a huge, dark freezer. "Ian's not here!"

Kevin headed for the front door and rang the bell.

After a couple of minutes, a muffled voice called, "Just a minute!"

Then the door swung open. Ian stood there with a bicycle spoke in his hand. "Hey guys! Come on in."

The X-crew kicked off their boots and piled their jackets on a bench in the hall. Then they followed Ian to his room in the back of the house. Ian's room was a converted garage. It was a large, awesome place with a five-foot-high platform for a bed and another platform for his drum kit. In another corner stood a work bench where Ian was working on his BMX bike. He was replacing spokes and truing his wheel, making sure it was perfectly balanced.

"My chain snapped and wiped out about a third of my spokes," Ian said.

Wall came up beside Ian and checked out what Ian was working on. Jamil went straight for the drum kit and sat on the stool behind it. "This is cool. Can I try it?"

"Sure."

Jamil picked up some sticks and started banging away.

Kevin trolled the room for handwriting samples. When he came to the desk, he casually pulled a few papers out of Ian's notebook. Every page was written in print instead of script. "Don't you write script?" Kevin asked casually, trying not to make Ian suspicious.

"Nope," Ian answered. He tightened a spoke. Then he spun his wheel on the truing mechanism to see if the wheel spun evenly. "My dad says mechanical engineers and architects all print and never write in script." He looked up at Kevin. "And I'm going to be an architect."

Nat and Kevin looked at each other.

Kevin shrugged. "Should we show him the notes?"

"Might as well," Nat replied. "If we're bringing Ella in to help solve this mystery, we might as well bring in everyone." She was still steamed that she had to work with her sister.

Kevin held out his hand. Nat gave him the notes.

"Ian, do any of these notes remind you of anything?" Kevin asked.

Jamil stopped banging on the drums and waited for Ian's reply.

"Like what?" Ian asked as he glanced at the notes.

"We don't know," Nat answered. "But the person . . ."

". . . or persons," Wall interrupted.

"Or persons who stole the trophy for the snowboarding comp left these notes for us," Nat explained.

Ian studied them for a minute. "Well, the notes don't make any sense at all."

"That's the way we feel," Jamil sighed. He had come out from behind the drum kit and joined the others.

"What about the handwriting? Does it remind you of anyone's?" Nat prodded.

Ian looked at the notes again. Suddenly, he laughed. "Yeah, it reminds me of my mom and dad's handwriting."

"What?" Nat blurted. "It couldn't be their handwriting."

Jamil slapped his forehead. "Now I'm totally confused."

"No, that's not what I mean," Ian replied. "This note." He held up the first note. "This one looks like the way my dad writes. It's really cramped and messy." Then he pointed to the second note. "While this one is very neatly written. My mom writes like this. The person who wrote this must have gotten an 'A' in penmanship."

"Now I get what you mean," Kevin said, as a light-bulb went off in his head. "Most girls write neater than boys. So you're saying that the first note was written by a boy and the second note by a girl."

"A left-handed girl," Wall corrected.

"So what we're looking for is a right-handed man and a left-handed woman," Jamil summed up.

"These notes *do* look like an adult wrote them," Nat added. "But where does that get us?"

"Back to your sister," Wall answered. "You're going to have to get help from Ella."

Nat slumped against the drum kit, lost her balance, and the whole kit came crashing down.

13

"Dad?"

"Just a second, Natalie," Mr. Whittemore said as he rang up a customer at the register.

The X-crew had hurried from Ian's house back to the Book Worm to look for Ella.

"Hi, Natalie," the customer said.

"Oh, hi, Mayor Masters," Nat responded.

"You solve any new mysteries lately?" the mayor asked. Mayor Masters had seen Nat and the crew solve an especially puzzling crime a few months back.

"We've got a new one now," Nat said. "Someone has stolen the trophy for the half pipe competition."

"And if we don't get it back, we have nothing to award the winner," Jamil added.

"That sounds awful," Mayor Masters said. "But I'm sure you'll solve it. You kids are crack detectives."

The crew smiled. They appreciated the vote of confidence.

Mr. Whittemore slipped the mayor's books in a bag. "That new novel is supposed to be a page-turner."

"I sure hope so," Mayor Masters replied. "See you kids later."

"Bye, Mayor," the kids replied.

"Now what's so important that you have to interrupt me while I'm with a customer?" asked Mr. Whittemore.

"We really need to find Ella," Nat said as she and her friends crowded around the front of the register.

"She's our only hope," Wall added.

Nat scowled at Wall. "Not exactly our only hope, but she's a good lead." Nat didn't want to admit that her sister might have the key to solving the mystery.

Mr. Whittemore smiled and crossed his arms. "So you don't really need Ella. Is that what you're saying?" He narrowed his eyes as he stared at Nat.

Sweat beaded on Nat's brow. Her dad was putting her in an awkward position—admitting that Ella's help was essential.

"Well, we do have some clues we could follow up on," Nat hedged. "We believe that the person who wrote the first note was a right-handed man and the second note was written by a left-handed woman."

"That's interesting," Mr. Whittemore conceded. "So where does that lead you?"

"I wish I knew," Nat admitted. "That's why we want to look at Ella's book."

"Ahhh! So all roads to solving the mystery now lead

through your little sister, do they?" Mr. Whittemore could hardly hold back his laugh.

"It's not funny, Dad," Nat protested. "If we don't find the trophy, we're sunk. We can't afford to buy another one."

"Uh, I think what your dad is saying, Nat," Kevin cut in, "is that you're going to have to include Ella on this mystery."

"Exactly! All roads lead through Ella," said Mr. Whittemore.

"No more dissing Ella," Jamil added. "We need her."

"And that means you need her, too," Wall told Nat.

Nat nodded, resigned to the fact that her little sister had something that she needed. "So, Dad, where is she?"

"I don't know, but she'll be home for supper," Mr. Whittemore answered. Then he looked at his watch. "Which should be in about an hour."

"What do we do now?" Nat asked her friends.

"Don't you have homework?" Mr. Whittemore interrupted.

"Parents," Jamil sighed. "They always think of the fun things to do." He picked up his knapsack. "Your dad's right, Nat. I better go home and do my homework."

Wall and Kevin followed, while Nat went upstairs to start on hers.

14

The bedroom was dark, except for a pool of light coming from the lamp beside Ella's bed.

Nat stood for a moment in the doorway and watched her sister read.

Ella lay stretched out on her stomach with her head propped in her hands.

"Ella?"

"Agh!" Ella fell out of her bed. She placed her hand over her heart as she stared at her sister standing over her. "You really scared me." She laughed. "I didn't hear you come in the room."

Nat smiled. "I hate when that happens." She sat down next to Ella and leaned against the side of the bed. "So what'd you find out?"

Ella reached up and pulled the book from the bed. "I'm not to the end yet."

"Can we read it together?" Nat asked.

Ella's eyes lit up and a broad grin spread across her face. "Yeah!" She leaned against her big sister and propped the book on her knees.

Nat put her arm around Ella and began to read the last chapter of *The Mighty Thompson Triplets and the Mystery of the Stolen Statue.* "Chapter Fourteen." Nat cleared her throat. "As Billy Thompson headed home from the market, he read the list his mother had written to make sure he hadn't forgotten anything. As he checked off everything he had in his bag, it suddenly dawned on him that his mother's handwriting looked more than a little familiar. He smiled as he realized he had seen his mom's handwriting in a place he'd never expected to see it—on the notes!"

Nat closed the book. "This doesn't make sense. If this story is the clue, then our mom is the thief. And that's just silly. She wasn't anywhere near the lodge when the trophy was stolen. She was at the store."

"But there must be some clue in the book that will lead you to the thief," Ella replied.

Nat stood up and put on her pajamas. "I'm going to bed. This Thompson Triplets clue is a total wash."

Ella sat on the floor disappointed. Finally, she got back on her bed, opened the book, and continued reading.

At breakfast Ella came skipping into the kitchen. She danced around the room and sang. "I know the answer. I know the answer."

"The answer to what, dear?" Mr. Whittemore asked.

"Why, to Nat's mystery, of course," Ella said with a smile.

"Really!" Nat said excitedly as she leaped from her chair and hugged her sister.

Ella beamed. "I figured it out after you went to bed," Ella explained. "Mom is the thief, but she didn't do it alone. Dad is the one who stole the trophy and Mom wrote one of the notes."

Mr. and Mrs. Whittemore laughed at this turn of events.

Nat stood there dumbfounded. "Why didn't I think of that?" Nat exclaimed. "Of course, Mom is left-handed. She could have written the second note!" Nat then turned to her parents. "Give it up." She held out her hand.

"What?" Mr. Whittemore asked, trying to suppress a smile.

"The trophy. Hand over the trophy," Nat answered.

Mrs. Whittemore wagged her finger back and forth. "It's not over yet. You still have to find the trophy."

"And you'll need Ella's help to do that," Mr. Whittemore added.

"You guys are so sick," Nat replied.

"We just want you to learn to appreciate your sister," Mrs. Whittemore explained. "You've been so hard on her lately that we thought you needed a lesson in valuing Ella."

Nat groaned.

Suddenly, Ella clapped her hands. "I know where

the trophy is," Ella said in a sing-song voice. She was thoroughly enjoying all of the attention.

"Where?" Nat asked excitedly.

"Meet me after school at the ski lodge and I'll show you," Ella said. She sat down and ate her cereal.

For the next half hour, no matter how much Nat begged, Ella wouldn't divulge her secret. She kept her mouth shut all the way to school.

15

"What's taking her so long?" Nat complained. She and the guys stood at the top of the steps leading into the ski lodge.

"Lighten up," Jamil replied. "The elementary school is farther away than the junior high." He stomped his feet on a step. He wasn't dressed warmly enough because he hadn't planned on waiting outside. "I think I'm going to have to go in and warm up soon."

"There she is," Kevin said as he pointed across the parking lot. Ella had just come into sight from around a van.

Nat cupped her hands to her mouth. "Hurry up!"

Ella waved and picked up her pace. She was dressed in a white snowsuit that made her look like the abominable snowman.

"Sitting through Mrs. Kirby's class this afternoon was torture," Wall said. "I thought I was going to die, I wanted to find that trophy so bad."

"I just hope Ella's right," Nat said skeptically.

"She's your sister, so she's got to be first rate," Jamil commented. He blew his warm breath on his ungloved hands.

Nat smiled. "I guess it's hard for me to see Ella's good points because she *is* my sister."

"You got that right," Kevin cracked.

Ella sloshed through the icy puddle at the bottom of the stairs leading to the resort's doors. "You won't believe where the trophy is."

"Where?" Nat blurted impatiently.

Ella stood as straight and tall as an eight-year-old can. "Follow me," she said formally.

The crew tromped behind Ella into the lodge. A blast of hot air blew into their faces as they entered. They all shed their jackets and hats.

"Jamil, I'm going to need your help," Ella said authoritatively, as she climbed out of her snowsuit and shoved it in her backpack.

Jamil smiled. "You sound like Nat."

Ella ignored his comment and headed straight for the stairs on the other side of the lobby. They all hurried down the stairs like they were playing follow the leader and Ella was now the leader. As they entered the locker room, Ella went straight to the locker rental desk. It was a counter against the far wall. A woman sat there reading a paperback novel and listening to her headphones.

"Excuse me," Ella said to the woman. Her face was barely above the edge of the counter. She flashed a winning smile.

The woman slid her headphones around her neck and set her book face down. She raised her eyebrows in a questioning look.

Ella then turned to Jamil. "This is where I need your help. We need to see who has rented lockers since the day of the robbery."

Jamil came up to the counter. "Laura, do you mind if I look at the sign-in sheets?"

Laura shrugged. From under the counter she pulled out a clipboard stuffed with sheets of paper and gave it to Jamil. Then she slipped her headphones back over her ears and started reading again.

"The silent type," Nat whispered to Kevin.

Kevin suppressed a laugh.

"I'm just glad Jamil's dad wasn't behind the counter. Then we'd never see the list," Wall added.

"Shhh! Don't give her any ideas," Kevin whispered.

Everyone crowded around Jamil to examine the sheets. Jamil flipped back to the day the trophy was stolen. About twenty people rented lockers that day. It was a slow day because it was a weekday in the middle of the month.

The page began with the name Nancy Castleburg, with the other names following below:

Robert Isle
Igmar Noble
Alice Montebalm
Jackson Pollash

Ethel Mowertail
Lisa Hilson
Will Williams
Rod McKeen
John Berrynut
Gary Donnelly
Maureen Cannon
Craig Kelman
Lateesha Fox
Andy Mayberry
J. D. Plant
Jimi Ensin
Sherman Avanti
Alonzo Ali
Jennifer Kadar

Jamil shook his head. "None of these means anything to me." He started to turn the page.

"Wait," Ella barked as she reached for the clipboard. She ran her finger up the list from the bottom and stopped at the sixth name from the top. "Here. This is it."

"Ethel Mowertail?" Kevin asked.

"Yes," Ella answered.

"Of course!" Nat yelled. "Oh, Dad is *so* sneaky. That's the name he came up with for Ella the other morning." Nat put Ella in a playful headlock and nuggied her head. "You're a real detective, kid sis!"

Ella laughed. "Yeah, Ethel Mowertail is Ella Whittemore mixed up."

"Oh, an anagram," Kevin replied.

"An ana . . . what?" Jamil asked.

"Anagram," Kevin answered. "That's when the letters of one word are mixed up to make another word."

"Exactly," Nat said. "But how did you know this, Ella?"

"It was simple," Ella explained. "The Thompson Triplets' stolen statue was hidden in their mom's locker at her aerobics gym. And the only lockers I knew of that Dad could use were the ones at the lodge here."

"Elementary, my dear Watson," Jamil added with a phony English accent.

"Now, how are we going to get in this locker?" Nat asked.

"Only one way," Jamil replied. "Ask my dad."

Everyone groaned.

"Fat chance he'll let us do that," Nat said.

"Let you do what?" Mr. Smith asked as he came down the hall from his office.

"Uh, Dad, could you let us in a locker?" Jamil asked.

"Which one?" Mr. Smith asked.

Jamil pointed to Ethel Mowertail's name on the list. "Locker 261."

Mr. Smith dug into his pocket and pulled out a key.

"Are you sick or something, Dad?" Jamil asked. "You never do this."

Mr. Smith laughed and went over to locker 261. As he swung open the door, the crew gasped. The snowboarding trophy was standing inside.

"I've been in on it from the beginning. I've just been waiting for you to figure it out," Mr. Smith explained.

Nat grabbed the trophy. "I'm not letting this out of my sight until after the competition." Then she turned to her sister. "You're the best, Ella. If only you weren't such a pain," Nat said, as she hugged her. "Thanks for your help."

Ella smiled and stuck her tongue out at her older sister. They both laughed.

"Uh, oh. I think Nat is being nice to Ella," Wall cracked.

"Get this on video," Kevin said. "We don't want her to deny it ever happened."

"Very funny," Nat said. "Come on, Ella. We've got a lot of stuff to do to include you and your friends in the snowboarding comp."

16

"Gravity pulls all boards equally. It's what you do with that pull that makes the difference," Nat said into the microphone. She was standing at the judges' table at the bottom of the half pipe. "Next up, the Mighty Mites division. Ages ten and below will compete for the title of the raddest, sickest rider still in grade school. These are the riders of the new era."

Scattered applause erupted from the audience that lined the edges of the pipe.

"First in the pipe is my home girl, Ella Whittemore!"

"Go Ella!" Mr. Whittemore shouted as he jumped up and down, cheering for his youngest daughter.

Nat smiled at her dad.

Ella dropped into the pipe riding regular. She had her hips and lower body aligned to the angle of the board while her head and shoulders shifted beyond the angle. She held her hands in perfect gunfighter position as she came down the near wall into the well of the pipe.

She came up the far wall and went air to fakie. This time she picked up some speed.

Nat held her breath. She was afraid that Ella might be going too fast to control her board.

But Ella zoomed up the near wall perfectly balanced and popped a nice Indy Air. She grabbed her board between her legs and came down regular.

"I didn't know she could do that," exclaimed Nat with surprise. The she gasped because she realized that she was still speaking in the mike. Everyone heard her. Total embarassment!

Ella shot across the well and floated up the far wall. Even though she was a foot or two below the lip, Ella caught some air and reached her front hand down to her toe edge. There was only time for it to brush the board's edge.

"Major Mute Air!" Nat announced. "She's setting the standard pretty high for the Mighty Mite division." Nat caught her dad's eye.

He nodded back and walked over.

Nat covered the mike with her hand. "Why, Dad?" asked Nat.

"I just thought you needed a lesson in appreciating your sister," Mr. Whittemore explained. "You've been riding her so hard lately that you had forgotten how much you could enjoy her."

Nat thought about that for a second, but not for long. Ella was demanding her attention in the pipe. Ella swooped up the near wall and pulled a smooth Pop Tart, going from fakie to forward without rotation.

"Sick trick!" Nat shouted into the mike. She was getting really excited and bounced on her toes. "My girl, Ella Whittemore!"

The spectators applauded.

Ella raised her hand in acknowledgment. Then she went big for her last trick. She came out of the pipe and double grabbed, frontside and backside.

"Excellent!" Nat exclaimed. "Ella Whittemore tops off her ride with a solid double grab." Nat then dropped the mike and ran to meet her sister.

They gave each other a big hug as the spectators cheered Ella's run.

XTREME LINGO

air to fakie: any trick where the wall is approached riding forwards, no rotation is necessary, and the snowboard lands riding backwards

alien soul: a grind on the insides of both skates so that your feet flare out like an alien spaceship

bonk: to crash

fishbrain: same as flying fish but performed on the ground

flying fish: while catching big air, extending the right leg, tucking the left, and grabbing the right skate

Indy air: a true "Indy air" is performed backside with the rear hand grabbing between the feet on the toe edge while the rear leg is boned

lu kang: while catching big air, reaching across your body and grabbing your opposite skate

McTwist: a 540-degree turn performed on a ramp. Named after Mike McGill

mute air: the front hand grabs the toe edge either between the toes or in front of the feet

pop tart: airing from fakie to forward in the halfpipe without rotation

roast beef air: the rear hand reaches between the legs and grabs the heel edge between the bindings while the rear leg is boned

tail grab: the rear hand grabs the tail of the board

unity: a cool grind where the skater's legs are crossed and the skates grind on the outside grind plates

Check out more rad lingo on ESPN's X Games website: http://ESPN.com